Home Sweet Home

Jean Marzollo

ILLUSTRATED BY

Ashley Wolff

HARPERCOLLINSPUBLISHERS

Home Sweet Home   Text copyright © 1997 by Jean Marzollo
Illustrations copyright © 1997 by Ashley Wolff   Printed in the U.S.A. All rights reserved.

Library of Congress Cataloging-in-Publication Data
Marzollo, Jean.
    Home sweet home / by Jean Marzollo; illustrated by Ashley Wolff.
        p.   cm.
    Summary: Illustrations and simple rhyming text ask blessings on everything on earth, from ant
to tree, stream to whale, and also on moonbeams and stars.
    ISBN 0-06-027562-6. — ISBN 0-06-027353-4 (lib. bdg.)
    1. Earth—Religious aspects—Juvenile literature.   2. Children—Prayer-books and devotions—
English.   [1. Prayers.   2. Earth—Religious aspects.]   I. Wolff, Ashley, ill.   II. Title.
BL438.2.M37   1997   96-35410
291.4'3—dc20   CIP
                                                                                          AC

Typography by Al Cetta   1 2 3 4 5 6 7 8 9 10 ❖   First Edition

DEC   1997

For Phoebe and Kirby
J. M.

For Jewell and Bud, with love
A.W.

Bless each bee

Each flower and tree

Bless each hare

Each fish, each bear

Each tender calf

Each tall giraffe

Bless each wren

Each rooster and hen

Each turtle
and snake

Each duck and drake

Bless each ant

Each cactus plant

Each dolphin and whale

Each little snail

Bless each foal

Each tiny tadpole

Each apple and pear
Each breath of air

Each lively stream

And quiet moonbeam

And bless each birth

In our home called Earth.